Promise Me

A Forbidden Billionaire AgeGap Romance

Billionaire Boy's Club
Book 2

Keke Renée

304 Publishing Company

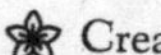 Created with Vellum

Disclaimer

THIS WORK OF FICTION contains strong language and explicit sexual content and is only intended for mature readers. This story contains unconventional situations, language, and sexual encounters that may offend some readers. This book is for mature readers (18+).

304 Publishing Company

WE SHOWCASE AUTHORS writing African American, Interracial, Women's Fiction, Urban Romance, Erotic, and Contemporary Romance novels. Along with Thriller, Suspense, Poetry, Beauty, and Style Books. Thank you for taking the time to visit. Join our mailing list to stay updated with new releases and blog posts.

Latest Releases by Keke Renée:

•Wet Heat (Wet Heat Series Book 1)

•Every Time We Touch Novelette (Wet Heat Book 2 Series)

•His Peace, Her Pleasure

•Baby, It's Cold Outside

•Love Don't Live Here Anymore, Vanessa Andrew Book 1

•Love Don't Live Here Anymore, Isabella Andrew Book2

•One Night Only—A Novelette (Love by Design Book 1)

•Cassian and Savannah (Love by Design Book 2)

•Deidra's Love (Love by Design Book 3)

•Protecting Bria (Special Force Operation Alphas)

• Sensual: A Brother's Best Friend Romance

• Seek To Please Book 1

• Seek To Touch Book 2

• Seek To Bare Book 3

• Seek To Love Book 4

Dedication

I WANT TO THANK FIRST the readers for loving these characters so much and waiting so long for them to come back.

Introduction

Are you signed up for my newsletter?

Join today and learn all the latest new releases, contests, giveaways, sneak peeks, and more.

https://BookHip.com/BKRPJL

Synopsis

Can I have power and love, or will one ruin the other?

During the day, I am a Senator.

A man of power abiding by the expectations set for me.

But at night, there is one place I can unwind and just be me.

Raya was supposed to be a distraction from politics and the pressures of my life.

Instead, she becomes an addiction. A force so seductive and sweet, I fall for her instantly.

I want to promise her a lifetime of love, but dating outside the boundaries threatens to destroy our love.

Will this forbidden romance endure, or will my career leave me hurt and alone?

Indulge in seduction in this new series from KeKe Renée. During the day, these billionaires are powerful tycoons who run the

*city, but at night, they come to Billionaire Boys
Club to play.*

Chapter 1

Remington

Loosening my tie, I drop it in the backseat and gesture for Arthur to relax while I head inside the club. I take the employee entrance because I need to stay under the wire to avoid anyone disturbing my peace and quiet outside of business. Passing down the hall, I go to the section reserved for me earlier today and sit in the back corner.

Removing my jacket, I grin at Sanya as she approaches my table with a frown. "What did he do this time?"

Rolling her eyes, she places my drink order and leans toward me to light my cigar. "Same as usual. Trying to boss me around," Sanya says with a sigh.

The employee door opens to the most beautiful woman I've ever seen, and a part of me feels like I should snatch her up and run away from here.

"Here you go, Sanya," she says, placing extra napkins on Sanya's tray.

Sanya takes out her iPad and starts typing, "Raya, I'd

like to introduce you to Senator Remington Ayton, an exclusive member, and Gerald's best friend."

Raya's eyes widen in shock. "Senator."

I extend my hand to take hers, lifting it to my mouth and kissing her knuckles. "Call me Remington."

"Oh, I can't do that," Raya responds shyly.

"You can and you will." My eyes train on her soft, sultry lips, smooth amber-brown skin, slender nose, and high cheekbones.

"Remington," Sanya calls my name.

I glance at her. "Bring another one. Raya, I'd like to buy you a drink."

Shocked by my statement, she looks between me and Sanya. "I'm working."

"Sanya wouldn't mind you taking a break."

"Actually, I do mind. I'm training her today," Sanya objects.

The music starts as the doors open, and Gerald strolls in, searching for one person and one person only. Everybody in the club knows it's Sanya. Gerald makes eye contact with me, and his frown clears when he sees Sanya talking to me. Marching over, he places a kiss on her cheek. He sits in the booth, and we shake hands.

"How long have you been here?" Gerald asks as he lights a cigar.

I ignore his question. "Tell your new employee that as the Senator, I should get what I want."

Sanya and Raya laugh at my comment as they head back to the bar.

Blowing out smoke, I lean back with my arm along the booth, watching Raya talk with Sanya. More than likely discussing me. "She's off limits."

Gerald chuckles at my statement. "You sound like me."

I narrow my eyes at him. "Good. That means you'll let every man here know that she's not to be touched."

"Raya's young."

"How young?"

"Twenty-five, I think."

I grunt, not expecting her to be in her mid-twenties. Her innocence intrigues me.

More women appear and head to each booth, checking on guests, while the main attraction stands off behind the mirror, showcasing her beauty. Gerald built the Billionaire Boys Club as an elite members-only space for clients who want privacy. Not a regular strip club but more a place for men to get together and remove the shield of everyday life. Some men take women home, but I've stayed away from that luxury until today. Raya has my mind and body ready to risk my job as a senator for one night.

Gerald frowns. "What's going on with you?"

I run a hand over my beard. "Fucking media is pissing me off."

"Probably not helping by hanging out with me."

"Being a billionaire bachelor doesn't help my image," I reply.

Raya walks past, chuckling at a joke from one of the guys in another booth. Leaning forward, I pin her with my gaze. She must sense my eyes on her because she looks up and clears her throat before taking their orders.

"Senator Falls." Cariss approaches the booth and leans forward to show her cleavage.

I nod. "Cariss."

Lifting my hand, she plants herself in my lap and crosses her legs.

"Cariss, you know we're not on that level."

She pouts and crosses her arms, "Every man in here would die to have a night with me,"

Gerald breaks out in laughter. I want to join in because Cariss delusional if she thinks I would be tempted, considering her reputation. Cariss is money hungry and looking to marry a billionaire. The last thing I would do is get caught in her web.

"Gerald, you know me well. Tell your friend I can be friendly and discreet," Cariss whispers, licking her lips.

"Cariss, your client is waving for you to get another bottle to their table. Keeping customers waiting is not good for business," Gerald reminds her.

Sliding off my lap, Cariss grabs her iPad and stomps off to work her section. I reach into my pocket for my ringing phone to see my assistant calling just as Raya and Sanya come back to refill our drinks.

"Sanya, come to my office quickly," Gerald requests, getting up and pulling her to the back.

* * *

Hours later, after finishing another drink, I head out of the club and back to my waiting car when I notice Raya standing by her car with the hood up. I jog over to her, and she jumps at my touch on her lower back.

"Car problems?"

Raya nods, holding her hand to her chest to calm her breathing. "I can't figure it out."

"It's too late to get a tow. Let me drive you home."

"Oh, I couldn't ask you to do that."

"Why not?"

"Because." Raya shrugs and leans in to grab her phone and purse.

"The place is locking up, and Sanya left hours ago with Gerald."

"I'm a big girl. I can find my way home."

"I don't doubt it, but I would feel better taking you. It's too late to get a driver service."

She looks over my shoulder at my limo. My driver flashes the lights, and she heads toward it.

"So all I needed to do was get my driver to confirm? That hurts," I tease.

Smiling, she shakes her head. I motion Arthur not to get out as she climbs into the back seat. Sliding in beside her, I introduce them.

"I don't live far from here." Raya clutches her purse in her lap.

"How old are you?"

She turns to look at me. "Twenty-two."

"Interesting."

"What about you?"

"Thirty-nine."

"You don't look old."

Chuckling, I press a hand to my chest like I'm hurt. "Ouch."

She shakes her head with a smile. "I didn't mean it like that. Old man."

"This old man could teach you a few things."

"Probably, but my mom warned me against men like you."

Moving close, my eyes fall to her lips, which part slightly. "What do men like me do, Raya?"

She exhales. "I-I... Senator Ayton."

"Call me Remington."

"Remington. I think it's best if we keep things professional between us."

"I disagree."

Her eyes sparkle, and my lingering stare causes her to cross her legs.

"We've arrived, Mr. Ayton," Arthur informs me.

I gesture for him to stay seated. Climbing out of the car, I walk around to open her door and extend my hand to help her out.

"Thank you," Raya says.

"You're welcome." I follow as she heads up the stairs to her apartment.

She turns to look back at me. "You don't need to walk me to my door."

"My mother taught me to be a gentleman."

She smiles as she slides her key into the lock. "Thank your mother for me."

I hike my brow. "Why?" I lean a hand on the doorframe and lean in close. "I plan to prove her statement wrong about men like me."

"Good luck, Mr. Ayton."

Caressing her cheek, I whisper, "Remington. Call me Remington, Miss Raya."

Chapter 2

Raya

Sanya's been a great help in training me as she starts to move into her new role of managing the other clubs for Gerald. I'm pushing myself to start back in school, but I hate relying on school aid or my parents for help with tuition, so I took a job at Billionaire Boys Club. What I didn't realize was the caliber of men who would be coming in and out of the club. The women I work with constantly fight and argue over specific tables to bag a rich guy.

"Do you hear me, Raya?" Mom asks, cutting across my thoughts.

She video-called me, and I listened with one ear as she complained about the price of the lemons she bought for the pie she plans to make for Sunday dinner.

"I'm here, Ma."

"Those girls have no common sense," Ma continues, moving on to her neighbor's daughters, who constantly fight outside.

"Ma, leave those folks alone." I place the phone on the

dresser and scoop my hair into a high ponytail before slipping my feet into my shoes.

"What time is your class?"

"I have an hour and still need to get my car checked."

"Maybe your dad can take a look at it today."

"No, that's too much."

"He's fine! You know he spoils you."

She's right. He does when it comes to me. My father would give me the world. My parents retired after years of working for the city. I visit mostly on the weekends because of my class schedule and working nights. Now that Dad's no longer working in sanitation, he gets bored and tries to do things around the house.

"Donna, leave that man alone," I tease, picking up my phone.

She glares at me for calling her by her first name. "Know your place, child."

I laugh at her frown. *I haven't been a child for four years.* "Yes, ma'am. I have to get going, Ma."

"Fine, Call me later."

"I will. Promise."

I hang up with Ma and grab my backpack and purse. My parents know where I work and hate my job, but I'm an adult and make my own choices. Wally and Donna weren't all bad growing up. I love them and appreciate their support and encouragement.

Locking my door, I stroll down the steps, texting back and forth with Sanya to plan a lunch date.

"Raya."

My head pops up, and my eyes widen as I see Remington waiting outside, leaning casually against the limo.

He tips his head toward the vehicle. "Get in."

I glance around nervously. He sticks out like a sore thumb in my Bronx neighborhood. "What are you doing?"

"Taking you to school."

My mouth opens and closes in shock. "Senator Ayton—"

"Either you get in the car, or I'll put you in it," Remington states.

I raise my chin in challenge, waiting to see what he'll do. He moves toward me, and I hastily get in and shut the door before anyone sees me.

"So childish," I huff, pulling on my seatbelt.

He smirks. "Glad you decided to listen."

I try to talk to him over the lump in my throat. "Listen, Senator Ayton—"

"Remington."

I grind my teeth in frustration. "Let me make myself clear, *Senator Ayton*. I'm not interested."

A grin splits his face. "You are."

"No, I am not," I snap.

"How are your parents? Wally and Donna, isn't it?" he asks suddenly.

My mouth drops open. "You're crazy."

"How is school going for you at Baruch College?" he continues, ignoring me.

I fold my arms over my chest. "None of your business."

"I have a few meetings on my schedule today, but afterward, I want to take you to dinner."

I know that men with money like him only care about showing off their little playthings. I haven't had many boyfriends, but being tossed aside is not on my agenda. "No."

"Give me one good reason why you won't go to dinner with me."

"Because I don't know you."

"Dinner will change that."

"I'm sure you have plenty of women who want to sleep with you. Why are you stalking me."

Laughing, he reaches over and grasps my hand as the car stops in front of my school. "Baby, I've never stalked a woman in my life. But you intrigue me, and I need to know why."

Slipping my hand out of his hold, I grab the handle and open the door. But before I go, I bend and look him in the eye. "That need is the problem. Senator Ayton, I'm not a shiny new toy for you to play with for a day or two to get your rocks off." I slam the door, ignoring the stares of the students around me as I stomp up the steps to the main building.

"Raya! Hold up."

I groan as I open the door and turn to face him.

"You forgot your purse, and before you open with that smart mouth of yours, I never said you were a new toy or an object. Before you judge, get to know me first, pretty lady." He presses a kiss on my forehead.

I'm acutely aware of students on us; a few even have their phones pointed our way, videoing us together. I'm embarrassed and flustered by his warm lips and addictive cologne that captures me in a trance.

* * *

Remington's muscular physique and strong hands distract me all day during classes. My teachers probably think I'm on something because my head is somewhere else, and I can't focus on any of the tests. I think about how he towered over me as he kissed my forehead, and I wondered how our lips would fit together, how he would taste.

"Are you going to eat your food?" Carrie asks, snapping me from my thoughts.

We're eating lunch after my classes, and Sanya and Carrie laugh at my confused state.

I shrug. "I'm not hungry."

"She's probably still hung up on her boyfriend," Sanya chimes with a laugh.

"Shut up." I stick my tongue out.

Carrie takes a few fries from my plate and pops them into her mouth. "Boyfriend? Ooh! Tell me all about him."

I sigh, letting them get their little comments out before I pin Sanya with my gaze. "Unlike you and Gerald, I'm single and happy. I want to avoid him altogether."

"When was the last time you went on a date?" Carrie asks me with a lift of her brow.

I lift my hamburger to my mouth and take a bite, wiping ketchup from my mouth. "Maybe six months or something," I reply.

"Girl, you need to do more than work at the club and go to school," Carrie scolds me.

Sanya nods in agreement. "Carrie's right, Raya. All you do is work and hang out with us."

Carrie nudges her arm. "What's wrong with us?"

I chuckle as she motions between the two of them.

"Raya, you're a beautiful girl, and I vote you go out with Remington to at least give him a chance," Sanya suggests. He's a good guy."

"He's a senator," I point out.

Carrie's eyes widen as she checks her vibrating phone. "Oh, shit!"

"What?" Sanya and I ask in unison.

Carrie glances at me and shoves her phone at Sanya.

"Raya, have you gone on social media today?" Sanya asks.

"No, why?" She hands me the phone, and I scroll through the posts. Senator Ayton is trending online. I open the video, and my mouth drops open. There's a video of *me* with the senator, and the angle makes it looks like we're kissing.

"I knew it!" Carrie whisper-shouts.

"You hooked up with him and never told me?" Sanya demands.

"No! He took me to class earlier today, and they got a clip of him kissing me on the forehead."

"Damn, he's sexy. I'd vote for him." Carrie grins, reaching for her phone.

I grumble and slink further in my seat, covering my face with my hands. "I knew somebody would see us."

Carrie grins. "At least he's cute."

I huff out a breath and remind her, "He's a Senator."

"So? He's a man, and he's single," Carrie replies.

Sanya nods. "She's right, Raya."

"My parents are going to kill me," I groan.

"Babe, you're an adult and pay your own bills," Carrie reminds me.

"And a college student trying to figure out my life and not looking for love."

"Who says you need to get married to the man? Fuck him and duck him." Carrie throws her hands in the air.

Sanya laughs. I flip her off and reach for my purse, leaving the money for my meal on the table.

"Where are you going?" Carrie asks.

"Home. I have to study and get some rest before work tomorrow."

"Can you host the book club tomorrow?" Sanya inquires.

"Fine. I guess."

Sanya stands to hug me. "Thanks, bestie. Call you later."

Chapter 3

Remington

Keeping my eyes forward, I listen to my assistant and chief of staff emphasize how my running around with a college girl is bad for my image and career. I've wanted to serve the public all my life, and getting into politics came easily because of my family's name.

The Ayton legacy goes back to my great-great-grandfather, a local mayor. Eventually, my father was groomed to become Governor, then Senator in New York. Now retired, all he does is take my mom on trips around the world and pressure me to have kids so they can spoil them. But I'm not hurting to have kids, and I don't see myself as a father.

I like the freedom to come and go as I please. Women come and go because I never stay long enough after we both get what we want. Spending money and taking them on trips is good for me, but they want commitment and marriage—two things I never saw in my future until Raya Rollins appeared at the club.

Halle, my assistant, taps her foot impatiently. She

scowls and releases a harsh breath. "Look, we don't say anything about you going to the club to let off a little steam, but it's becoming an issue," she mutters.

"My personal life doesn't concern you."

"I think I get to have a say when you throw your life away on some bimbo," Halle snaps.

My brow rises. When will she get the hint that I'm not interested in her? She's a good assistant, but she makes no secret that she wants more. I've told her plenty of times that I never mix business with pleasure.

"Halle, give us a minute." Kevin, my chief of staff, says. He tips his head toward the door for her to leave the office.

"Fine," Halle huffs.

Kevin waits for the door to shut, and I check the time on my watch. I told Arthur to be there around eight to pick up Raya and take her to the restaurant.

"What's the first thing I told you when running for office?" Kevin reminds me.

I sit back in my chair, my hands behind my head. "Try not to take a bribe."

Kevin sighs. "No. I believe it was don't embarrass yourself or jeopardize your career for a woman."

I rise from my seat. "Raya's not an embarrassment, and if you say shit like that again, prepare to look for another job." I pick up my briefcase and jacket and walk out of the room. "I have to leave."

"Where are you going?"

"Out."

"We need to figure out how to navigate the media."

"That's your job. I have plans."

"Remington, it's not fair for you to leave a mess for us to fix." Kevin trails behind me.

We halt at the elevator, and I press the button for the main lobby. "So they caught me with a woman I like."

"She's half your age and not up to standards," Kevin mutters.

"I'm going to pretend you didn't just say that shit to me. Being a Senator and a businessman won't stop me from kicking your ass." I gently slap him on the cheek.

The doors open, and I step into the waiting elevator as Halle glares at me. I wave good night. I leave the building and head to my SUV with my security. After getting in the back, I decide I don't want to head home to change clothes and have Raya try to get out of dinner. Instead, I have my driver take me straight to the restaurant.

"Sir, I have Arthur on the line," one of my security guys passes me his cell phone.

"Yes, Arthur?"

"Sir, she refuses to go," Arthur says.

Chuckling, I check the time and see it's almost seven forty-five. "Where are you?"

"Outside her apartment."

"Tell her if she doesn't come outside in the next five minutes, she'll have an eviction notice on her door."

"Yes, sir," Arthur responds.

A minute later, I hear Raya yelling and screaming on the other end of the phone.

"She said you can kiss her ass." Arthur chortles.

Her feisty spirit causes my dick to harden behind my zipper.

"Thanks, Arthur." Hanging up, I direct my men to take me to her place. On the way there, I call the restaurant to have the food delivered to us.

* * *

Minutes later, the car arrives outside her apartment with the catering van behind me. I ask the caterer to give me a few seconds. Arthur stands on the steps near the door.

"She's still here?" I ask.

"Yes, and refuses to answer the door."

"Thanks. You can take off." Knocking on her door, I slide my hands in my pockets and wait for her to answer. "Open the door, Raya, or else."

"Go away!"

"Pretty lady, I want to look you in the eye when we have a conversation."

"Nothing to talk about."

"I can have the entire block shut down, and everybody will know it's because you hurt my feelings."

The latches on the door move, but she holds the top lock to keep me outside. "You're bluffing."

Grinning, I lean against the door. "Try me."

Raya grimaces and shuts the door. A few seconds later, it opens wide. I wave to the staff to come inside with the food. Walking past her, I remove my coat and lay it on the couch.

"What are you doing?" Raya hisses, trying to stop them from bringing in the food trays.

"The food will get cold if you keep holding them up."

"Remington, really?"

"Raya, yes."

"Please leave! He's not in charge!" Raya snaps at the caterers.

I move close to take her hand, but she jerks away. Before she can protest, I lift her and carry her down the hallway to the nearest room. I shut the door behind us and push her against the wall, blocking her from leaving. "Stop fighting me."

She lifts her chin, meeting my gaze. "You're stalking me."

"Baby, I'm far from a stalker, but if you like that shit, I can play that role."

She shoves me, but I don't move. I grab her wrists in one hand and pin them above her head.

"Quit playing around, Remington. My face is online for the world to see, and they're saying I'm your new floozy."

"We both know that's not true."

"It doesn't matter. You need to leave me alone. My life was peaceful before you."

"And my life got better the second I laid eyes on you."

She tenses, locking her gaze with mine. "What are you doing?"

"I like you."

She shakes her head. "You're crazy."

"You should have never worked at the club."

"How is working at the club my fault?"

Tugging her shorts, I tell her in a firm voice, "You're too sexy."

She slaps my hand. "Don't touch me."

"Come on. Let's eat. My stomach is growling."

"Are you seriously making me eat dinner with you?"

"Well, I had a date planned at a restaurant, but you refused to go, so I brought the restaurant to you."

"Money doesn't impress me, Remington."

"That's one of the reasons I like you. My lifestyle doesn't impress you."

"We're different, Senator. Our worlds would never fit."

I tug her into the living room. "We have a lot to discuss, but let's have dinner first."

The air is heavy with the aroma of smothered pork chops, creamy roasted red pepper pasta, and salad. Candlelight softly glows, and a bottle of champagne sits in the middle of the table on ice. I help Raya into her seat and take my place at the other end of the table. The catering staff places our plates on the table.

"Food looks great," Raya says.

I stare at her beautiful face. "Food's not the only thing I want to eat."

Blushing, she lowers her head and cuts into her food.

I pop open the champagne bottle and pour a glass for us both. "Tell me about yourself."

"I'm surprised you don't already know my social security number," Raya snarks.

"That smart-ass mouth needs something long and thick to occupy it instead of the food on your plate."

Raya chokes, and I laugh and wait for her to compose herself.

"Beyond this dinner, nothing is going to happen between us," Raya announces.

It's cute that she thinks we'll only have one night together. "You know what? I think you like pushing my buttons."

"Please don't flatter yourself."

I don't want to push her further, so I leave once we've finished dinner. I grab my coat and kiss her forehead while the staff finishes cleaning her kitchen.

"You're leaving?" Raya looks disappointed.

"Yeah, I have an early meeting tomorrow."

"Oh, right. I have class, and then I'm working at the club." Raya follows me to the door.

I turn to say goodnight, feeling the heavy pull of

attraction between us. My next actions will cause her to admit she wants me or end what could've been.

Slowly, I lean in, staring at her lips. I brush my tongue over her top lip. She moans and presses her hands against my chest, sucking my tongue into her mouth. My dick stirs in my pants, and that's my clue to pull back.

"See you later, Raya."

Smiling, she holds two fingers against her lips. "You too, Remington."

"Not Senator Ayton?"

She smiles. "Go before I change my mind."

I chuckle as I jog to my car.

Chapter 4

Raya

A few nights have passed since my date with Remington. He hasn't called me in three days. And I'm kind of pissed that he's avoided me. I know it's crazy to be upset, but the moment our lips touched, I felt sparks. My entire body wanted him. I wouldn't have controlled myself if he'd stayed any longer at my place, so I was glad when he decided to leave before anything sexual happened.

Pushing my jacket and purse into my locker, I saunter to the vanity seat to freshen up my makeup. I'm applying a coat of lipstick as Sanya comes in with our assignments for the day.

"Hey, babe. You have four tables."

I sigh. "Thanks, Sanya."

"What's wrong with you?"

"Tired," I answer in a matter of a fact tone.

Sanya stands beside me and leans against the wall. "That face tells me differently."

"Sorry. Long school day."

She looks me up and down. "Well, cheer up, buttercup. Your man is outside."

My eyes balloon in surprise. "What?"

"I knew it!" Sanya shouts.

"Stop screaming, girl!"

"Did Remington piss you off?"

"No."

Shutting the door behind her, Sanya sits on the desk. "Spill the beans."

"Nothing to spill. And is he really here?"

"Yes, and before you demand I change your tables, he requested to be in your section."

I sigh heavily, slip on my heels, and check my hair. "He can request all he wants. I don't care."

"Oh, you like him?"

I stand to push my breasts into the corset top. "Sanya, I am not some little girl with a crush."

"Tell me what he did, or I'll go out and ask him."

I stomp my foot. "Okay, okay! He hasn't called me since our date."

Sanya smirks. "And you're mad because you think he doesn't like you or he's playing games," she says astutely.

I nod. "Please keep it between us."

"Why are you embarrassed?"

"Because being in a relationship scares me, especially with someone of his caliber. Look at me."

"Yes, you're so terrible," she says sarcastically. "You're a sexy, beautiful, intelligent woman who could have any man she chooses."

I pick up my iPad and pen and head to the main floor. The staff is stocking the bar. The doors open, and Sanya greets guests.

I smile as two men walk in and sit at one of my tables. "Hello, gentlemen. Welcome to Billionaire Boys Club."

One of the men has a wide smirk. I flush when he reaches out to touch my hand. "I hope you come with the cigars."

"She doesn't."

I tense at the familiar deep voice of the man who's been avoiding me since our first date. I turn to face him with a glare.

"Remington, what's up, man?" My customer reaches to shake his hand.

Remington ignores him, grasps my hand, and marches us to his section.

I snatch away from him and watch as he sits. He has the nerve to grin at me as if he hasn't avoided me for days.

"You have a bottle girl, Senator Ayton." I turn to leave.

"Stop."

I freeze at his command.

"Turn around, Raya."

His eyes are heavy with appreciation as I slowly turn. "You don't get to demand my time when you've avoided me for days."

"I didn't think you noticed."

"See that cocky shit? You can keep that."

"All right. I apologize."

I drink in his powerful presence. "Someone will be over to take your order."

"Sanya put you on my table."

"No, she didn't."

"Check your updated tables."

Stifling through my iPad, I notice the red mark

attached to my section and click it to update. It now shows I'm only scheduled to manage Remington's table.

Scowling, I stomp over to the bar and slam the iPad on the top. "Are you kidding me?"

Sanya mutters into her headset, telling someone to hold on. "Why are you yelling?"

I point at Remington and back to the iPad. "You changed my tables."

"Raya, calm down. He paid a little more to have you exclusively."

"That's not fair."

"You know you want him to pay attention to you. All the pouting you've done about missing him, and now he's here."

I huff, clutching the iPad and pen.

"Go work and leave me alone." Sanya waves, laughing at my predicament.

Somehow, I'll pay her back for setting me up. I close my eyes and tell myself to stay calm.

I take a deep breath and head to Remington's section to see another guest has joined him. "Hello, I'm Raya, your bottle girl for the evening. What can I get you?" I ask, pasting on a smile.

Remington lights the cigar and blows out smoke. "Mike, this is Raya, the woman I told you about."

"Raya." Mike points at me and laughs.

"Excuse me?"

Mike places his hand on his chest. "Sorry, little momma. Sorry. My boy told me you'd be pissed when he came today."

I shrug. "I'm not sure why he thinks I'd be pissed."

"Can I get the aged bourbon?" Mike asks.

"Of course. Coming right up. And for you, Mr. Ayton?"

Remington's jaw flexes in annoyance. "My usual. And Raya?"

I ignore him and turn to leave, but before I can escape, Remington captures my elbow. Goosebumps spread across my skin, and my breathing stutters at his warm touch.

"Dinner at my place."

"No, thank you."

Mike bursts into laughter, and Remington flips him off. "Arthur will be here to pick you up. I know your car is still messed up."

"Sanya is my ride home," I remark, not wanting to be alone with him.

"Sanya has a prior engagement with Gerald and asked if I would bring you home," he replies.

I ignore his statement and head to the bar to get their drinks. For the rest of my shift, I try to figure out how to get out of tonight. But I'm also curious about how the bachelor senator lives and if all of his women get a gift after having sex.

* * *

"Sit," Remington says.

Looking up, I see him staring back at me with determination as he slides his tongue across his upper lip.

"What are you doing?" I cross my arms over my chest and narrow my gaze on him. It was a bad idea for me to go to this dinner with him, especially in such a tight dress that barely covers my breasts and ass.

Remington cocks his head to the side. "I invited you to dinner."

"Why?" Men like him only want sex. I promised myself I would focus on my goals and leave love alone.

"Because we have some unfinished business to discuss."

"I won't stop working at the cigar bar," I say before the subject comes up.

Remington pulls out my chair and bends to whisper, "Did I ask you to quit?"

"I know your type, Remington."

Remington takes his seat. He lifts his champagne glass. "Let's toast."

I wrap my fingers around my glass. "To what"

"To enjoying each other's company."

Sitting back in my seat, I cross my legs. "Nothing is going to happen between us."

Remington sips his champagne. "I apologize for not getting back to you sooner. It's good to know you're not immune to me. As soon as you walked in, your gaze found mine. Your lips are aching for me to kiss them and make you mine."

"I don't accept your apology."

His lust-filled gaze trails up my body. "Then let me apologize another way."

I can't deny that Remington is hot. Why shouldn't I enjoy a night in his arms?

* * *

After the night with Remington, I let Sanya talk me into hosting the book club at my place. The girls pick a dark romance by L.K. Ryan, and the possessive hero in the book reminds me of Remington.

I can't focus on the discussion about the hot love scene because my night with Remington is replaying in my head. How his tongue stayed in my pussy all night long, and he never requested anything in return. A part of me wanted to protest when he drove me home. I thought of his thick, hard dick all day during classes, and I'm still thinking about it now.

"What are your thoughts, Raya?"

"It's great," I say absently.

Sanya giggles and waves a hand in front of my face. I put the book on my lap and give Sanya my attention.

"How was it?"

All eyes are on me. "Sanya, I am not talking about my love life."

"He must have really put it down," Carrie teases.

"We haven't had sex," I mumble.

"What?"

I throw my hands in the air. "We haven't had sex!" I rest my head back on the couch.

"Not even a peek?" Carrie teases.

"Ugh, I hate you guys."

"Our girl is sex-deprived," Sanya jests.

"Who are you dating?" another girl questions.

"Nobody." I shut the conversation down, not wanting my business to be the topic of discussion for the rest of the afternoon.

My phone dings, and I check it to see a text from Remington.

Remington: *A car is picking you up in an hour.*

Me: *How did you get my number?*

Remington: *A question you don't need the answer to, Raya.*

Me: *Stalking is not a good look, Senator.*

Remington: *Stalking? You had no problem with my tongue in your pussy last night.*

"Raya, are you listening?" Sanya asks.

Me: *You talk a big game, Remington. I doubt you can keep up.*

Sanya swipes my phone. "'I doubt you can keep up.'" Sanya reads my text out loud.

"Give me my phone, Sanya." I snap, trying to grab it.

Making kissing faces, Sanya hands me the phone and playfully smacks my ass. I stick my tongue out at her and head off to figure out what to wear for a date.

"Raya, make sure you shave!" Sanya yells after me.

Chapter 5

Remington

I stare down at Raya's silky, radiant body. I can't imagine a woman as stunning as Raya. Rubbing a hand over her smooth skin, I capture her lips, keeping her underneath me. She pants as my tongue snakes into her mouth, sucking on her plush lips. Nibbling on her neck, I make a point to leave a mark so everyone knows she's mine. The shines bathes the room as I slip my hand along her warm throbbing pussy.

"Oh, God!" she yelps as I stroke her with my fingers.

"Let me explore you, baby," I encourage, peppering kisses over her chest and nipping her breasts.

"Remy, please," Raya whimpers,

She quivers when I trace a path down to her sleek arousal. Spreading her legs wider, I remove my finger, and Raya sucks it into her mouth. I'm ready to search for her pleasure points.

"Shit," Raya pants.

She arches her back, cupping my head as I circle her with my tongue. Hearing her moans and whimpers is music to my ears.

"Fuck me," she begs.

Swirling my tongue and dipping my thumb into her asshole, I take her to another level, and she crushes my head between her thighs.

I chuckle and come up to let her taste her essence before pushing forward at her entrance.

"Shit, Raya," I grunt, easing out and plunging deep.

Her tightness has me in a chokehold as I pump in and out. She gasps as my bare chest covers her. She wraps her arms around my neck, and my gentleness turns into punishment at the thought of someone ever being this close to her. Reclaiming her lips, I quicken my pace, making the headboard hit the wall.

"I'm going to come, Remy."

"You've been a bad girl keeping my pussy from me," I growl, slapping her thigh. I press her breasts together, ravishing and admiring my new friends.

Throwing her head back, Raya succumbs to a shuddering climax. She parts her lips in satisfaction. Once her orgasm subsides, I stroke faster to catch my nut. My toes curl, and my spine stiffens as I release. Running her hand over my chest, Raya shimmies down and takes me into her mouth.

"You know what you're doing?"

Ignoring my question, she surprises me with her control and gag reflex, twisting and rotating in opposite directions as she bobs her head up and down. Her eyes never leave mine, and I let her have her way, watching saliva ooze from her mouth.

"Raya, you know you're never leaving me, right?"

Grinning, she sucks on my balls, hollows her jaws, and relaxes her throat. I feel my soul leave my body.

"Raya!" I clench my teeth, about to bust all over the bed if she doesn't move.

"Mmmm...." Raya moans, sucking the last drop of cum.

Pulling her up, I shove my tongue down her throat, not caring she still has my essence in her mouth.

* * *

Holding the door open, I take Raya's hand, and we walk out of the store, eating ice cream and admiring the local sights. Not much for sweet things, I pass mine over to her and watch her eat the two scoops of chocolate. Squeezing her to my side, I drop lingering kisses on her cheek.

We continue to the car going to the villa. My security has the place surrounded if we need them, but everyone knows me around here and allows me privacy. A few times, paparazzi have shown up, but the locals give them fake stories to throw them off.

"What are you thinking about?"

I smile. "You."

"About me sucking your dick or something else?" Raya teases.

I observe her in sweet amusement. "Both."

She punches my arm. "Asshole."

"Baby, you asked. But seriously, I'm enjoying our time together."

"Me, too."

"I wish we didn't have to go back."

"Yeah, work and school are already a hassle with me being here for one day. Staying longer would cause more problems."

"Gerald knows you're here."

"He's not the issue. Me missing out on money. That's my problem. Next semester won't pay for itself."

"I can cover you for this weekend."

Raya shakes her head as the car arrives at the villa. "No."

"I asked you to come and want to ensure you're compensated."

"I appreciate the thought, Remington, but it's too much."

I pull her close. "It's never enough where you're concerned."

Sighing, she eases out of my hold. "We have the rest of the day. Let's have dinner on the balcony and watch a movie."

"Avoiding the question won't make it go away."

"I'm not avoiding anything."

"You are, but for now, you can have your little tantrum." I slap her butt and kiss her forehead.

Watching a movie lasts for twenty minutes before we find ourselves wrapped up in each other in bed again. Raya buries her face against my throat as I grip her ass cheeks in my callused hands and spread them wide. My heartbeat skyrockets as her sweet moans fill the room. Rocking back and forth, her gasps of pleasure tell me how turned on she is.

She rides my dick, her expression revealing how much she wants to please me. Bouncing her rounded ass, she rotates her hips. "You feel so good."

I apply pressure to her clit. "Take what belongs to you, Raya."

Her skin glows and sweat sprinkles her chest. She

leans forward, arches her back, and slams down on my pole.

"Fuck, girl!"

We come together, riding the pleasure until we're exhausted and out of breath. Dinner will have to wait.

Chapter 6

Raya

"Raya, are you dating Remington Ayton?" a girl in class asks while the teacher hands out the latest quiz.

"What?"

"It's all over the news and social media." She presses her phone and passes it to me. I hear the moans of two people having sex.

"Hey!" the teacher yells.

The girl laughs with her friends. I'm so embarrassed and don't wait for the class to be dismissed. I grab my backpack and run from the room and out of the building. I bump into someone and drop my books.

"Are you Raya Rollins?" a woman asks.

"Who are you?"

"I'm with Channel Four News." She holds up an ID badge.

I gather my books and start to walk away.

"Hey, wait!"

"Raya!"

I look ahead to see Remington by the limo holding the door open.

I want to avoid everybody, so I head for my car when the keys are snatched out of my hand.

"Give me my keys!" I bark.

"Get in the car."

"No."

"Raya, you're not driving alone."

"I don't give a fuck. Leave me alone."

People are staring, which only intensifies my annoyance with him. Uncaring how it looks, he throws me over his shoulder and walks to his limo.

"Are you crazy!" Pummeling his back does nothing, and I'm pretty sure I could get arrested for hitting a public figure on camera, with everyone recording the situation.

Remington places me in the backseat and shuts the door. I scoot to the corner in a huff.

"My house, Arthur," Remington commands.

"Yes, sir," Arthur answers.

"Arthur, take me to my apartment," I demand.

He looks in the rearview mirror, and Remington shakes his head.

"He works for me," Remington reminds me.

"Fine. I'll call a cab from your place."

"No, you won't."

"We'll see about that."

* * *

Hours pass, and Remington stays glued to the telephone while our sex life is replayed on social media and news stations. It had to be one of the staff members who recorded us and showed it to some blogger for a few thousand dollars. My parents call, and I refuse to answer, but they leave messages to call back. Sanya sends messages telling me I should sue everybody. But the damage is done, and money can't fix my life being plastered all over the news.

"You need to eat," Remington begs me, his eyes full of concern.

"Not hungry." For a moment, I want to give in and forget being upset.

"Raya, baby," he implores.

"Save it. I need to go home."

"It's safer for you here."

"Says who?"

"My chief of staff. And me."

"I can handle myself."

"Why should you when I'm here?"

I stand to leave the room. "This is all your fault!"

"It was my assistant," he mutters.

I raise my eyes in alarm. "Repeat that. Clearly, I didn't hear you right."

"My assistant leaked the tape."

"Some jealous bitch you slept with?"

"We never had anything."

"But she wanted you, right?"

His eyes darken as he holds my gaze.

Remington can make any excuse in the book. For him not to say anything about her wanting him in the past pisses me off.

"Can I go now?"

"I told you, Raya, we need to stay here at least until the dust settles and my staff can prepare a statement," he reminds me impatiently.

Avoiding further conversation, I go to the guest bedroom and call Sanya. At least she'll be on my side.

"How are you feeling?" Sanya asks.

"Ready to disappear."

"It will blow over in a day or two."

"He said the same thing," I say, my voice heavy with frustration.

"He's right."

"He's the reason we're in this mess."

"Remington didn't leak the tape."

"No, his assistant did it because she wants him."

"You sound mad that he never slept with her."

I'm irritated. "I never should have gone out with him in the first place."

"Listen, he called me and said you'd be staying there for a day or two, and I think he's right. I bought you some clothes and left them there for you."

"When did that happen?"

"On your little getaway. He let me use the black card. Honey, he's a keeper," Sanya whispers.

I hear muttering in her background. "Tell Gerald I'm sorry for interrupting you guys."

"He'll be fine. You're my bestie."

"I guess I should call my parents and get the yelling done for the night."

"Please! Like your parents never did anything spontaneous."

"They haven't."

"Parents were our age once, Raya. Get it together, babe." Sanya jests.

We say our goodbyes and end the call.

"Come down to eat." Remington startles me, standing at the door in black slacks and a white t-shirt.

"You're not going back to the office?"

"No. I have everything here in my home office. We need to talk."

"Okay, I'm coming."

His chef has a feast laid out for us. I can't hold onto my anger any longer. I know it wasn't him. He had a crazy assistant.

I walk into his arms, lean forward, and kiss him. "I'm sorry."

He rubs his hand along my back. "Sorry for what?"

"Taking my anger out on you."

"I'm sorry that bitch caused you embarrassment. I fired her, and the police are filing charges. And I've sent flowers and a card to your parents."

I lean back and stare at him in surprise. "How? What?"

"Baby, I plan on being with you and want the best for you."

"When did you have time?"

"Your man's got skills," he jokes.

"Funny. Can I have my keys back, please?"

"Tomorrow." He dips his head for a kiss.

"Why tomorrow?"

He cups my ass. "Tonight, I want to show you how sorry I am."

Chapter 7

Remington

A week later.

Watching the reporters retract the footage and apologize for the leaked sex tape and seeing my assistant in handcuffs gives me the satisfaction I need. Being single and high profile doesn't mean I'll stick my dick into any woman who flirts. My parents raised me with standards, even though being a playboy gives people the impression all I do is fuck and leave them high and dry.

Lighting the cigar, I take a pull, letting the stress ease from my head as I listen to the music. Raya, as usual, tends to my section in the club, and I watch her work refilling the ice and setting the rest of the guys' drinks down. Gerald, Mike, and two other friends came today to celebrate my early numbers for reelection. At first, Raya was hesitant when I asked her to attend a fundraiser with me to make things public. Since our situation became common knowledge, we've been closer than ever.

"You need a refill, Remy?" she asks, and I nod.

"Raya, he can refill his own drink," Mike chastises.

I feel sorry for him. His girl dumped him a few days ago because she caught him cheating.

"Leave him alone, Mike," Raya hisses.

Pulling her into my lap, I pass the cigar to her to take a pull. She straddles me, positioning the cigar between her plump lips and blowing the smoke in my face giving me a shotgun. It's the sexiest thing we've done since our trip.

"What time are you off?" I ask, running a hand up her back and gripping her neck.

"Around two am, baby."

"Gerald, she needs to leave at ten."

Raya jumps off my lap. "No, sir. I have to study tonight."

"You can study at my place."

Laughing at me, she says, "Studying at your place will happen when there's ice water in hell–never."

"You've been around Sanya too long," I fuss.

She chuckles at my frown and kisses me softly. "I promise the weekend is all you and me."

"Bro, you in love?" Mike wonders.

"Yeah, why?"

"Looks good on you," Gerald says.

"All my boys are getting women and settling down," Mike observes.

"Maybe you're next."

"Doubt I can keep my dick to one woman." Mike glances down, and all three of us burst into laughter.

I give him a grudging nod. "Man, get the hell out of here."

Mike grins and focuses on Gerald. "How is the opening of the club?"

"Going good. Should be ready in a few months. Your investments are coming along," Gerald informs me.

"Glad to hear." I glance over my shoulder to look for Raya.

"Imagine if the press discovered you invested in this place." Mike laughs.

"Nothing wrong with my business," Gerald snaps.

Mike smirks. "It's like a playground for men with half-dressed women."

"The women don't strip, and they make a decent living. They may dress a little sexier, but my club is professional and classy," Gerald states.

"Well, let me go find one of these classy women to get me a refill."

"Raya will be back," I suggest.

Mike jumps up. "No offense, but your girl is cock blocking, bro."

* * *

Raya's weekend surprise blows me away when she charters a boat and has Arthur drive us to the dock on her dime. I tell her to never spend money on me again and reimburse her for the expenses.

Under the blankets on the deck, we watch the sunset, eat lunch, and listen to music. We talk about our plans once we get back to the city and Raya finishes for the semester. I plan to have my staff help with her schedule so we can spend as much time together as possible. I also want to support her in her career. I want her to be the best she can be.

Walking into Billionaire Boys Club that afternoon led me to the love of my life. I didn't expect it, but now I can't live without the happiness that Raya brings into my life. I have no problem spoiling her and letting the world know she belongs to me.

Lounging on the deck, Raya smiles as she looks at the diamond necklace around her neck. I had it hand-crafted and planned to give it to her when she finished school, but today just felt right.

I rip her bikini off and spread her pussy lips, smelling her arousal. Gripping her legs, I pinch her thigh and ease my finger in and out. I press a kiss there to ease the sting as she rocks back and forth on my tongue.

"I love my surprise," I mumble against her flesh.

She moans. "Me, too."

I ease my dick into her tight pussy, closing my eyes to savor the moment.

"Remington," she breathes.

"Tell me your thoughts, baby."

"I can't."

"Yes, you can. We're not going anywhere."

Her juices cover my thighs as I slowly stroke in and out. I can sense her wanting me to pick up the pace. Her sex faces have me in a trance.

"Oh, God, Remy. It's too much," she stutters.

"Come on, baby. This your dick."

Her eyes pop open and widen in surprise. Then she grins. "Yes. All mine."

"Damn right."

Raya's inner walls grip my dick, and I know I'm headed for a release that may wreck me. Her breathing hitches, and I push her flat on her back. She grasps my thighs, her moans growing louder as she meets my thrusts. I pray the crew doesn't hear us.

"Remy, right there!"

"You coming for me, baby?"

"Yes! Please let me come."

"Take all of my dick. You can handle it."

Her nails prick my skin as she tenses and falls over the edge. I follow immediately, holding her close as we come together.

I fall on top of her, gasping for breath. "Damn."

Raya giggles as she runs a hand through my sweaty hair. "Damn is right,"

* * *

I hope you enjoyed Raya and Remington's story. Also, check out the next book in the series, "**Consume Me**," a best friend's brother's romance coming up next.

Have you checked out "**His Peace Her Pleasure?**" Click here https://books2read.com/u/3JJroP a billionaire, steamy romance.

Also, steamy romance that includes bodyguard tropes, one-night stands, marriage troubles, and more here *"**Seeking In Romance 1-6**"* https://books2read.com/u/4ELGLe

Don't forget if you love Fling romances, bodyguard, and forced proximity, then check out "**Protecting Chanel**" https://books2read.com/u/mqwPB8

If you love brother's best friend romance, you'll love "**Sensual**" **here** https://books2read.com/u/49lYYM with a dash of steamy romance.

Check out Bodyguard Romance, military, romantic suspense here *"**Protecting Bria**"* https://books2read.com/u/bQJkjd

Follow college romance and more characters in *"**Taste**"* here https://books2read.com/u/bpz1Ng

How about a steamy, medical romance? Check out **"Haven"** https://books2read.com/u/4jAvyZ a steamy, enemies-to-lovers romance.

Please also check out my ***"Love Don't Live Here Anymore Vanessa Andrew"*** https://books2read.-com/u/mBOWGZ a steamy curvy girl, enemies-to-lovers romance.

Follow that up with a workplace vacation romance in **"Love Don't Live Here Anymore Isabella Andrew"** https://books2read.com/u/brVNO7

More workplace, boss romances with **"Love by Design Box Set 1-3"** https://books2read.com/u/m2ldEk

Reader Questions

1. Should Remington and Ray get married?

2. Was Remington's staff wrong for trying to break him and Ray up?

3. Is the age difference a big problem Raya and Remington?

4. Would you like to see more of Remington and Ray's family?

5. Should Remington keep his private life away from the cameras?

About the Author

A TENNESSEE NATIVE and California dreaming Author KeKe Renée, is living and striving to continue her passion for writing short story romances in genres ranging from Erotic, Paranormal, and Women's Fiction.

What's Next?

WANT TO KNOW WHAT HAPPENS next?

Follow me on Bookbub and social media today.

Reviews are the lifeblood of the publishing world. They're read, appreciated, and needed. Please consider taking the time to leave a few words wherever you buy books. Sign up for updates and sneak peeks at the site below.

Acknowledgments

I CAN'T MENTION ENOUGH the support and dedication of my author buddies for keeping me uplifted. My behind-the-scenes team of beta readers, editors, designers, and more. As a writer, I continue to strive for the best, and I appreciate each and every person who reads my work. Without your continual feedback, I wouldn't be on this path, letting doubts slip away.

Catalog of Releases by Keke Renée:

•Wet Heat (Wet Heat Series Book 1)

•Every time We Touch Novelette (Wet Heat Book 2 Series)

•His Peace, Her Pleasure

•Baby, It's Cold Outside

•Love Don't Live Here Anymore, Vanessa Andrew Book 1

•Love Don't Live Here Anymore, Isabella Andrew Book 2

•One Night Only-A Novelette (Love by Design Book 1)

•Cassian and Savannah (Love by Design Book 2)

•Deidra's Love (Love by Design Book 3)

•Protecting Bria (Special Force Operation Alphas)

•Protecting Chanel (Special Force Operation Alphas)

•Haven

•Taste (A New Adult romance)

•Sensual

•Seek To Please

•Seek To Bare

Catalog of Releases by Keke Renée:

- Seek To Touch
- Seek To Love
- Seek To Trust
- Seek To Earn
- Protecting Yanira (Special Force Operation Alphas)

Thank you so much for reading. If you enjoyed the crazy ride and want to leave a review, we'd truly appreciate the support.